W9-BFI-455

Cookie Soup

and Other Good-Night Stories

By Michaela Muntean

Illustrated by Joe Ewers

On *Sesame Street* Luis is played by Emilio Delgado

A SESAME STREET / GOLDEN PRESS BOOK

Published by Western Publishing Company, Inc., Racine, Wisconsin 53404

BIG BIRD AND THE LOST BEAR

One of Radar's button eyes hung loosely on a piece of thread. His coat was dirty and a bit of stuffing was coming out of one of his ears.

"You don't look very well," Big Bird said as he carefully tucked his blanket around the little bear. "You had better stay in bed until I get back from play group." Big Bird patted Radar on the head. Then he waved good-bye and hurried to play group.

It was a busy morning. The class made sculptures out of clay. They colored pictures, played with blocks, and sang songs. It was Grover's turn for show-and-tell. He had brought a book about baby animals, and the teacher read it to the class. When she finished, she said, "Big Bird, next week it is your turn to bring something for show-and-tell."

"Oh, good!" said Big Bird. "I would like to bring my teddy bear, Radar." Then he remembered how Radar had looked earlier that morning. "Except he hasn't been feeling very well," said Big Bird sadly.

"Maybe he will be better next week," the teacher said.

"Yes," said Big Bird, "maybe he will." But for the rest of the morning, he couldn't help thinking about the little bear waiting for him at home.

When Big Bird got home from play group, he called out, "Radar, I'm back!"

But Radar wasn't there!

Big Bird looked under the blanket. "I'm *sure* I left him here," said Big Bird, scratching his head.

He looked in the nest again. He looked in his toy box and every drawer in his dresser. He looked on top of things and behind things and under things, but he couldn't find Radar.

Big Bird was worried. "Where could he have gone?" he said. He thought about Radar's button eye hanging on the piece of thread, and the stuffing coming out of his ear.

"That bear is in no shape to leave the nest. If I have to search every inch of Sesame Street, I will find him," said Big Bird.

On Sesame Street, Big Bird
asked everyone he met if they had
seen Radar. He asked the mail carrier,
the garbage collectors, and a truck
driver. But every answer was the
same, and that answer was no. No
one had seen Radar.

Big Bird did not give up. He
asked Oscar, Ernie, and Bert. He
asked at Hooper's Store, and at
Luis's Fix-It Shop.

He looked inside a telephone booth, on top of the mailbox, and under benches. He looked everywhere he thought a bear could be, but he did not find Radar.

Big Bird walked sadly down the street. As he passed the Wash and Dry Laundromat he glanced in the window. What he saw made him stop and hurry inside.

"Granny!" Big Bird cried.

"Big Bird!" Granny cried, giving him a hug. "I thought I'd surprise you and come for a visit. Radar didn't look too well, so I fixed him up and gave him a bath. I hope you weren't worried about him."

"I was," said Big Bird. "But I'm not anymore!"

Radar's button eye was sewn in place, his ear was mended, and he was soft and fluffy-clean.

"Oh, thank you, Granny!"

Big Bird gave Radar a big bird-hug. "I have a surprise for you, too, Radar! Next week you can come to play group with me."

COOKIE SOUP

When Ernie returned home from playing in the park, Cookie Monster was waiting for him.

"Congratulations," cried Cookie Monster. "Today is your lucky day. Me here to make dinner for you!"

Cookie Monster headed straight for the kitchen.

Ernie followed him. "But, Cookie," he said, "I don't think we have anything to make dinner *with*. We haven't been to the grocery store yet."

"Hmmm," said Cookie. "This is big problem, but luckily, me here to solve it for you! Do you have cookie?"

Ernie looked in the cookie jar. There was one oatmeal cookie left.

"COOKIE!" said Cookie Monster. "Just what we need to make cookie soup."

"*Cookie soup?*" asked Ernie.

"Yes," said Cookie. "It is delicious old Monster family recipe. You will love it. First we need big pot."

Ernie found a big pot.

"Now we need water in pot," Cookie Monster said, and Ernie filled the pot with water.

Soon the water in the pot was bubbling on the stove, and Cookie Monster dropped the oatmeal cookie into it. In a few minutes, he tasted it.

"Mmmm," he said. "It is good, but it could use some salt and pepper." Ernie handed Cookie Monster the salt and pepper shakers, and into the simmering pot with the oatmeal cookie, Cookie Monster added

a pinch of salt
and a dash of pepper.

Cookie stirred and tasted the soup again. "We have to wait for flavor to cook in," he said. "While we wait, me look around."

He looked in the cupboard and found one onion and two potatoes.

"ONION! POTATOES!" he cried. "They will make cookie soup even better!" And into the pot with

 the oatmeal cookie,
 a pinch of salt,
 and a dash of pepper

he added:

 one big red onion and
 two round brown potatoes.

While the soup simmered on the stove Cookie Monster looked in the refrigerator. "You told me you had nothing to eat!" he cried. "But look at this! TOMATOES! CARROTS! CELERY!

"These will make cookie soup taste delicious," Cookie said. And into the pot with

      the oatmeal cookie,
      a pinch of salt,
      a dash of pepper,
      one big red onion, and
      two round brown potatoes

he added:

      three red ripe tomatoes,
      four long orange carrots,
      and five green stalks of celery.

Cookie Monster stirred the soup again. "What else have you got in refrigerator?" he asked.

"There's some pickles and mayonnaise…"

"Pickles and mayonnaise not good in cookie soup. Anything else?"

"Well, there's some leftover roast beef," Ernie said.

"ROAST BEEF!" cried Cookie Monster. "Why you not tell me this right away? Roast beef will make cookie soup best soup ever!" And so into the pot with

the oatmeal cookie,
a pinch of salt,
a dash of pepper,
one big red onion,
two round brown potatoes,
three red ripe tomatoes,
four long orange carrots, and
five green stalks of celery

he added:

six juicy slices of roast beef.

The soup began to smell good. Cookie Monster stirred it and tasted it. "It is ready! Now we eat *big* bowl of cookie soup."

Ernie tasted the soup and said, "You're right, Cookie. This cookie soup is delicious! I can't wait until Bert comes home. He'll never believe that we made this whole pot of soup with just one cookie!"

NEVER ASK A HONKER
TO SPEND THE NIGHT

"I, Grover, am here to give you some advice. It is very good advice, so listen carefully. Never, and I mean *never*, invite a Honker to spend the night at your house.

"Now, you may ask why. It is a good question, and I, Grover, will tell you the answer. It is because Honkers honk.

"From the minute they get to your house, they honk. They honk hello to your mommy. They honk while you help set the table for supper. Then they keep right on honking even while they eat!

"They honk while you help your mommy clear the table. They honk while you play checkers. They honk while your mommy makes popcorn for you, and then they keep on honking right through your favorite television program!

"When it is time to get ready for bed, they do not stop honking. They honk while they brush their teeth and comb their fur. They honk while they put on their pajamas. They honk as they climb into bed. They even honk while your mommy is reading you a good-night story!

"But here is the worst part. Even after they are asleep, they do not stop honking. It sounds something like this: *honk-honk-shoooo, honk-honk-shoooo.*

"There is no way, and I mean *no way,* to block out that sound. You can try wrapping your pillow around your head. You can try wearing earplugs. You can even try sleeping out in the hallway, but nothing works.

"So that is why I, Grover, after saying good-bye to my Honker guests, am such a tired little monster this morning. Please remember this good advice, and never, ever, ever invite a Honker to spend the night at *your* house."